JUMPING JACK

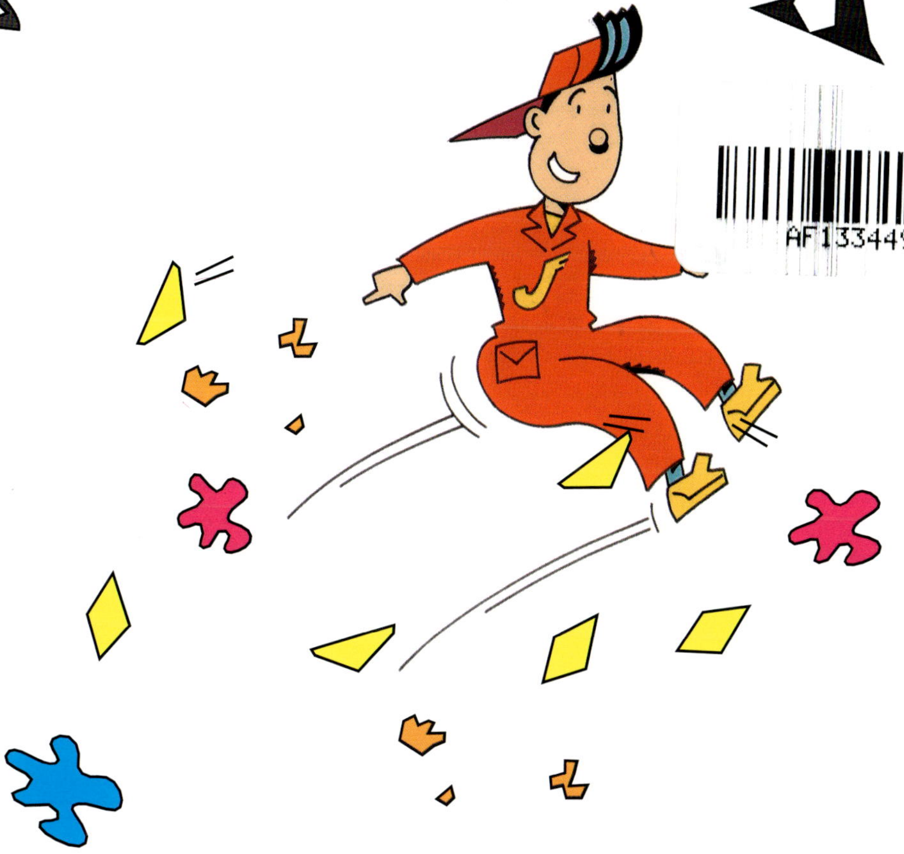

Julia Donaldson
Illustrated by Colin Mier

Mum was out. My big brother, Dave, was watching TV. I was playing a computer game called Jumping Jack.

In the game, Jumping Jack was looking for his dog. He was jumping around everywhere. He jumped from hill to hill, then he jumped from reef to reef, but he couldn't find his dog.

Today, Jumping Jack got to another level.
He jumped over volcanoes and dinosaurs,
but he still couldn't find his dog.

Jumping Jack went to the next level. He saw his dog, but the dog was locked up in a house. Jack had a rusty old key. He put it in the lock but it didn't fit. Jumping Jack was so angry that he jumped up and down all over the screen.

Suddenly, he jumped right out of the screen and on to my desk. He knocked over a box of disks.

"Hey!" I shouted.

Jumping Jack paid no attention. He jumped off the desk, down to the floor, and out of the room.

I followed him into the kitchen. Jumping Jack jumped up on to the table. He knocked over a pot of jam.

"Stop!" I shouted.

Jumping Jack jumped up into the cupboard. He jumped about and made a great mess. He spilled the coffee. He knocked over some cans.

Then he put a bottle into his sack.

"What's that?" I asked.

Jumping Jack paid no attention. He jumped back to the table and down to the floor.

Then he jumped out of the kitchen and up the stairs. I followed him into the bathroom.

Jumping Jack jumped into the sink and out again. I tried to grab him but he jumped up into the bathroom cabinet. He spilled Mum's shampoo and knocked over my brother's shaving cream.

Then he put a bottle into his sack.
"Hey! What are you doing?" I shouted.
But Jumping Jack was off again.

He jumped back down the stairs and into the workroom. He knocked over the tool box and spilled some paint. Then he grabbed a can and put it in his sack.

"Stop that!" I shouted, but Jumping Jack was off again.

I followed him back to the computer. He jumped on to the desk and back into the screen. Just then I heard a car drive up. Mum was back!

"What's all this?" she asked when she saw the mess in the kitchen.
"Jumping Jack did it!" I said.

"Oh no!" said Mum when she saw the mess in the bathroom.

"It was Jumping Jack," I said.

"Look at this mess!" shouted Mum when she looked in the workroom.

"Jumping Jack made the mess, not me!" I said.

Just then my brother called out, "Mum, Tess, look at this!"

He had stopped watching TV and was watching Jumping Jack on the computer instead.

Jumping Jack had just taken something out of his sack. It was a bottle.

"Hey," said Mum. "That's my cooking oil!"

Jumping Jack poured some oil in the lock and tried the rusty key. It didn't turn.

He took another bottle out of his sack.
"That's my bath oil!" said Mum.

Jumping Jack tried the bath oil, but the key still didn't turn.

Jumping Jack looked in his sack again.
"That's the tool oil!" said Dave.

Jumping Jack poured a drop of the tool oil in the lock. He tried the key again. This time it turned in the lock.

Jumping Jack opened the door of the old house. Out ran his dog and jumped into Jumping Jack's arms!

Then Jumping Jack turned around and looked at us. He had a big smile on his face.

"Thank you for the oil!" he said.

"Thanks to you I got my dog back."